Story Time for Little Monsters

The Littlest Werewolf's Story

Written by Rusty Fischer
Illustrated by Joel Cook

magic wagon

visit us at www.abdopublishing.com

Published by Magic Wagon, a division of the ABDO Group, PO Box 398166, Minneapolis, MN 55439.
Copyright © 2014 by Abdo Consulting Group, Inc. International copyrights reserved in all countries.

Looking Glass Library™ is a trademark and logo of Magic Wagon.

Printed in the United States of America, North Mankato, Minnesota.
102013
012014

♻ This book contains at least 10% recycled materials.

Written by Rusty Fischer
Illustrations by Joel Cook
Edited by Stephanie Hedlund and Rochelle Baltzer

Cover and interior design by Renée LaViolette and Candice Keimig

Library of Congress Cataloging-in-Publication Data

Fischer, Rusty, author.
   The littlest werewolf's story / written by Rusty Fischer ; illustrated by Joel Cook.
      pages cm. -- (Story time for little monsters)
   Summary: In rhyming text, Little Wolfie tells his mother about his adventures until he finally falls
asleep.
   ISBN 978-1-62402-021-6
1. Werewolves--Juvenile fiction. 2. Mothers and sons--Juvenile fiction. 3. Bedtime--Juvenile fiction.
4. Stories in rhyme. [1. Stories in rhyme. 2. Werewolves--Fiction. 3. Mothers and sons--Fiction. 4.
Bedtime--Fiction.] I. Cook, Joel, illustrator. II. Title.
   PZ8.3.F62854Lj 2014
   813.6--dc23   2013025327

The littlest werewolf jumped into bed
and his mother tucked him in tight.
"But I'm not ready," he whined and squirmed,
"to be tucked in all snug for the night!"

"That's nonsense," Mother Wolfie said, as she patted and petted his fur.
"You love your nightly lullaby, of that I am absolutely sure!"

Little Wolfie rolled his big, brown eyes. "It's not your lullabies of which I'm tired," he said as his mother scowled at him. "It's just that I'm still quite . . . wired!"

"Of course you are," she said to him. "You've had quite an adventurous day!" "That's just it." Wolfie grinned at her. "I still want to run out and play!"

"Not now," she said, smiling down at him.
"Even wolf boys need their rest!"
"But, Mom," he whined, as he tossed
and turned, "today was just the best!"

His mother thought, then she gave an idea that was sure to make our Wolfie sleepy. "Why don't *you* tell *me* what you did today, and don't hold back on the creepy!"

Now Little Wolfie's eyes grew wide. "You mean it?" he asked Mother dear. And when she said that indeed she did, our Wolfie smiled from ear to ear.

"It all started at the zoo," he began, with a wicked little grin. "Which was quite a challenge at first, you see since of course they wouldn't let me in!

"But I snuck around back, for a sideways attack, and slipped through a hole in the gate. And once inside, Mother dear, how I ate and I ate and I ate!

"But I was just getting started. That zoo was far from the main course. And even after all the cages were empty, why, I could have eaten a horse!

"And, Mother dear, that's just what I did. Yes, horses were next on the menu. So I scampered over to Avery's Stables and ate everything but the very last horseshoe!

"And then I was thirsty, so thirsty you see. So I drank 'til the lake bed was dry. And the fishes were flopping and flapping their tails, so I thought a few dozen I'd try!

"Those fish, they were tasty, but tiny, you see. They left an empty feeling inside. And as the townspeople were after me by now, I figured I'd best run and hide!

"And what better place, Mother dear,
to hide out than a barn full of cattle?
I swallowed them whole after one
monstrous werewolf versus cattle battle!

"But the townsfolk, they would not give up.
So I roared until my throat was sore.
And when they still would not let me be,
I roared and roared, then roared some more.

"And finally, they ran away–
the people of this town.
And that was when I finally
started *really* chowing down!

"I gobbled every cat in town
and then ate all the frogs.
When I'd scarfed up all the squirrels,
I wolfed down all the dogs!

"And then, just to spice things up, I had a dozen pedicures. And while sitting there I shed enough to make a dozen furs!

"I tore a dozen shirts in half and split through all my drawers. I went through 16 tennis shoes while racing around on all fours."

The little werewolf paused
his tale to stifle a furry yawn.
And Mother Wolfie smiled to
see that his energy was gone.

He snuggled in his covers tight
and closed his weary eyes.
He replaced his storytelling skills
with contented, little sighs.

"Your leg I'm not trying to pull.
You'll need energy for tomorrow night,
when the moon is actually full!"